DUCKLING

Kamila Shamsie

WITH ILLUSTRATIONS BY

Laura Barrett

HaymarketBooks

Chicago, Illinois

ONCE UPON A TIME, there was an egg that would not hatch. The mother duck had started off sitting on nine eggs, and now there were eight newborn ducklings clustered around her crying out, "Peep peep" and one egg beneath her, larger than the others, without the tiniest crack on its surface. "Quack quack," the mother duck said to the eight ducklings, telling them to be patient and stay close to her on the bank of the river, in the shade of the burdock leaves. The ducklings pecked at each other and at themselves, eager to see the world beyond—the slow-moving river, the fields stacked with bales of golden hay, the farmhouses where non-duck creatures roamed about, mooing and purring and singing—but unwilling to leave their mother's side.

A stork came along on its stilt-like legs and bent its long neck toward the duck. "Let me look at that egg, and I'll tell you what to do," the stork said, but the duck pretended not to understand the stork's accent (it had flown in from Egypt). The stork tried again, but although the duck tried not to be rude to anyone, particularly in front of her ducklings, she worried what ideas this stork might have brought with it from far away, and once again pretended not to understand. "Hmph," said the stork and flew off with such a mighty beating of its wings that all the little ducklings tumbled over in the breeze it created.

"Rude creature," the duck said, helping the ducklings back on their feet (they were all rolling about, having never learned to do anything else while in their shells). An old duck waddled along and asked what was going on. The mother duck told her about the egg that wouldn't hatch.

"Probably a turkey's egg," the old duck said. "I sat on one once, and it took forever to hatch. And then out came a turkey speaking gobbledygook, and no matter what I did it wouldn't ever enter the water. What a waste of time. Let me look." She prodded the duck's folded wing with her bill, prompting her to stand up (because a well-behaved younger duck mustn't ever be rude to an older duck). The old duck peered be-tween the mother duck's legs. "Hmm. I don't like the look of that. Must be a turkey."

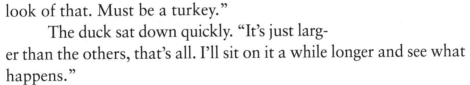

The duck sat down quickly. "It's just larg-er than the others, that's all. I'll sit on it a while longer and see what happens."

"Suit yourself," the old duck said. "But don't expect any gratitude from that creature when it hatches."

A little while later there was a cracking sound. The ducklings rolled around with excitement, and one tumbled all the way down to the river and fell in with a SPLISH! The mother duck hastened down to retrieve the wet thing, all the ducklings following her in a row, crying out "PEEP PEEP," so no one saw the moment when the egg broke apart and the youngest of the ducklings emerged, eyes scrunching shut against the newness of light and then springing open to take in the wonder of the world. "So much to see," thought the youngest of the ducklings, even though the only thing in her field of vision was a burdock leaf and a little bit of sky.

She turned her head, and now she saw her mother and her eight duckling siblings. They were looking from the broken shell to

her and back to the broken shell as if trying to understand the relationship between the egg and the hatched creature.

What the mother duck saw was this: not a duckling with feathers the color of the sun on a brilliant summer day, but one that looked like clouds when they begin to fill with rain, announcing that cold misery will soon follow. The darkness of the duckling's feathers intensified in her bill and webbed feet—but at least the feet were webbed, thought the mother. If she could swim, she was a duck and no turkey.

And so the next morning, when the sun shined bright in the sky, the mother duck led all nine of her ducklings toward the water. SPLASH! she went in, and SPLISH SPLISH SPLISH SPLISH SPLISH SPLISH SPLISH SPLISH SPLASH, the others followed. The youngest of the ducklings was also the largest, you see, and so she made a SPLASH rather than a SPLISH as she entered the water. Each of the ducklings went down under the surface of the river, and each one bobbed right back up, and all of them quickly started to move their webbed feet so they weren't merely staying afloat but actually swimming toward their mother. The mother duck saw that the youngest of the ducklings moved the fastest and carried herself in the most

upright manner, and she knew that this child of hers might not look like the others, but she was a fine duckling and one of whom any mother could be proud.

A little while later the cats and the cows and the ducks on the farm near the river saw the mother duck and eight little similar-looking ducklings and one larger different-looking duckling walk into the farmyard in a more-or-less straight line. The mother duck instructed her babies to be particularly nice to the Grand Old Duck who lived on the farm, because he was the most important duck of all—so important in fact that the farmer had tied a red tag to his leg as a mark of his prestige.

"What is that?" said the Grand Old Duck, riding out of the barn on the back of a cow. He pointed his red-tagged foot at the raincloud-colored duckling. "The rest of you can stay, but I'm not having that thing in my farmyard. It hurts my eyes to look at it."

"I know she looks different, but she can dive into the river and fetch you eels for dinner," said the mother duck.

"If that's true she can stay," the Grand Old Duck said. "Make sure she doesn't bring me stringy eels."

Once upon a time, all the eels in the river were plump, and there were plenty for every duck, but now the countryside was being taken over by factories, and the rivers were drying up. Fewer rivers meant fewer eels, and fewer eels meant the once-generous ducks looked suspiciously at newcomers and calculated how much each one would eat, even though ducks can eat a variety of things, and there was no rule that said eels had to be part of their diet. But the Grand Old Duck, who could have used his authority to instruct the younger ducks to share the juicy slugs and the succulent river plants and the crunchy insects and the slurpy fish-eggs, thought only of his own eel-loving belly. And that belly was, if truth be told, a much bigger belly than any duck should have, which is why the Grand Old Duck couldn't go to the river to find his own eels anymore but needed to bully newcomers into bringing the eels to him.

And so, every morning, the raincloud-duckling would start her day by diving into the river and searching for the plumpest eel for the Grand Old Duck. On the first morning, the mother duck went along with her to instruct her how to dive deep, how to find the hiding places of eels, and how to catch hold of one and bring it up to the surface. The duckling learned quickly, and very soon she didn't need her mother's instructions, but the mother duck continued to go down to the river with her every morning and search along the riverbank for worms for her own breakfast and algae and tadpoles for her ducklings. On the way to and from the river, the mother duck would tell her youngest duckling stories about The Duck Who Couldn't Fly, in which the heroine was a young duckling who always

proved herself to be stronger, braver, and more intelligent than all the other ducks, who laughed at her for the unusually formed wings that prevented her from taking flight. In each story, The Duck Who Couldn't Fly found a way to save the other ducklings from some calamity, and eventually they stopped laughing and learned to appreciate her for what she was rather than what she was not.

The raincloud-duckling loved this time with the mother duck, but the other ducklings began to be jealous of the youngest sister, who received more attention from their mother than they did. And the Grand Old Duck, who should have been grateful to the raincloud-duckling, came to despise her, because every time the duckling walked into the barn with a plump eel in her bill she reminded the Grand Old Duck of the days when he was young and fit and could fetch his own breakfast, and it was easier to hate

the duckling than to hate the duck he had become. So the Grand Old Duck started to curse and peck at the raincloud-duckling, and then the other little ducklings began to do the same. The cats and the cows thought that there must be something very wrong with the raincloud-duckling, otherwise why would the other ducks treat her this way? So they, too, started to claw and kick and hiss at the poor young creature, and soon everyone started to say that this duckling was not right: "Look at her feathers look at her feet look at the way everyone hates her WHY IS SHE HERE WHY IS SHE AMONG US THIS WRONG WRONG DUCKLING?"

The mother duck always defended her youngest duckling, and that made the other ducklings and cats and cows fall silent. But one day, it was the Grand Old Duck who was yelling insults at the raincloud-duckling when the mother duck came hurrying out of the barn and said, "Don't say things like that, she's just a baby, and she brings you an eel every morning." All the feathers stood up on the Grand Old Duck's neck, and he and the cow he rode on turned to the mother duck, hissing and lowing, and said, "MOO QUACK WHY DID YOU BRING HER HERE QUACK MOO WHAT KIND OF DUCK HATCHES A WRONG WRONG DUCKLING LIKE THIS QUACK HISS MOO WHAT KIND OF WRONG WRONG DUCK ARE YOU?"

After that the mother duck went very quiet and no longer defended her raincloud-duckling and stopped going out to the river with her. And then the day came when the other ducklings were pecking at her and the cat was clawing and the cow was slapping her head with its tail while the Grand Old Duck warbled, "YOU WRONG WRONG DUCKLING," and the raincloud-duckling saw her mother and ran to her . . . and her mother cuffed her with one wing so that the duckling was knocked off her feet. And as she lay there, that poor unloved duckling, she heard her mother say, "I should never have hatched you."

The duckling remained there, on the pitted rough ground, for a very long time. It was only when all the creatures of the farm had gone into the barn for the night that she stood up, shook her feathers, and without a single look back at the barn (where she would have seen the mother duck watching her through the window) took a few quick steps and flew over the fence that separated the farm from the field beyond. She flew further than she knew her wings could take her, and at last, when she could go no further, she stopped on a great wild moor, by the edge of a swamp, hid her face under her wing, and slept.

She was woken in the morning by a chorus of quacks. Some wild ducks of the moor had gathered around and were trying to decide what to do about this newcomer. She lifted her face out of her feathers, and the wild ducks jumped back in surprise. "You're an ugly one, aren't you?" said a wild duck, shaking his head so that his green feathers shimmered beautifully. The smaller duck standing next to him added, "Why, none of our young drakes would ever want to marry you!"

The duckling didn't know why anyone would say a thing like this. What kind of duck looks at another duck and thinks about who would or wouldn't want to marry her? She didn't want to be married. She wanted a place where she could dive in the river and not be pecked at or laughed at or, worst of all, left all on her own while the other ducklings joked and talked and chewed on river reeds and swam in lazy circles together.

The duckling sighed and hid her face under her wing again. The wild ducks moved on. A day went by—two days. She roused herself only to drink water from the swamp and eat insects that hovered near its surface amid the tall

reeds. But then, on the third day, the world changed. Along came two young geese—a brother and sister pair of goslings—as the duckling was watching insects dart about, wondering if she would spend the rest of her life in this muddy swamp among the mud-colored reeds. "Halloo!" they honked. "Who are you, and why are you here all alone?"

The duckling told them she had left home to find some place better, and one of the goslings said, "You're an adventurer, like us!" And the other gosling said, "Don't you think you'd better come along with us? An adventure shared is always a better adventure."

"Yes please," said the duckling, rising to her feet in excitement.

Pa-POW! Ker-chick. Pa-POW!

What was that sound? The goslings' eyes opened wide, they fell onto their sides, and didn't get up. Pa-POW! Pa-POW! Pa-POW! More shots sounded, and a flock of geese that had been lying in the reeds all rose up in the air and one by one crashed down. The duckling looked this way and that. Where to go? What to do?

All around the swamp, on the marshy ground and up in the spreading branches of trees, hunters fired and reloaded, fired and reloaded. Everywhere, smoke and gunshots and an acrid scent. Then there was a new sound, a sharp bark, right behind our duckling. She turned her head, and there was a dog, its mouth full of sharp, cruel teeth. It thrust its head toward the duckling, saliva dripping from its jaws.

The duckling shut her eyes tight so that she wouldn't have to see the dog's mouth closing on her neck, ending her life. But the dog merely sniffed at her and then bounded away toward a fallen goose.

"I'm such a wrong wrong duckling that the dog can't even bear to bite me," the duckling thought. "And I'm certain the hunters won't even want to kill me." So thinking, she flew up and streaked

across the swamp, across the moor, far away from the sound of dying geese and the acrid smell of gunpowder.

Soon, a storm blew up. The clouds burst open and poured down rain. Thunder rumbled and roared, lightning split the sky in two. The wind and rain buffeted the duckling this way and that, making it impossible to fly or even to see. She had no choice but to drop down to the ground once more and hide under the branch of an oak tree. There she wiped the rainwater out of her eyes with her wing and looked around.

A short distance away was a collection of timber piled higgledy-piggledy. It was a wonder it hadn't scattered in the storm, which was showing no sign of easing up. Just then, a light came on from inside the pile of wood, and the duckling saw that it was a little tumbling-down-but-still-standing house that appeared to have been lifted up by a cyclone and then dropped back down onto the ground at an angle, so that the whole structure was leaning to one side and looked as if it might at any moment tip over. The window shutters and the front door were half off their hinges, flapping in the wind.

The duckling thought about staying under the oak tree until the storm passed, but the wind was blowing rain down between the branches, and it was all so very miserable that the duckling put aside her fear and crept in through the flapping front door.

In this house lived an old woman with a goat she called Lofty Cudchew and a cat she called Chablis Furball. When she saw the duckling walk in, the old woman cried out, "A duck! Perhaps she can lay some eggs for my breakfast. Let's keep her a few weeks and see if she does."

And so the duckling was allowed, if not exactly welcomed, into the house. She soon learned that the goat and the cat thought themselves the most wonderful creatures in the world. The cat spent its days licking its own fur, and the goat rubbed its chin against the walls of the house until its beard gleamed. "Look at us, look at us!" they would say. "Aren't we beautiful? Aren't we glorious?"

They had a song they liked to sing together, and it went like this:

GOAT:
You can travel over land and sea
You'll never see a goat like me
Such elegance, such poise
Everybody enjoys
The sight of this goat and his gleaming goatee

CAT:
You can travel over land and sea
You'll never see a cat like me
So purr-fect, so debonair
Doesn't it fill you with despair
To know you'll never be that fine feline: Chablis

GOAT AND CAT:
You can travel over land and sea
From the Amazon to the old Yangtze
You'll never see the likes of us
You'll never be the likes of us
So grovel, serve, and worship us, ducky

"It isn't very nice to show off," said the duckling, and the cat arched her back and said it wasn't showing off if you were merely stating a fact.

"Anyway," said the goat, "you haven't laid an egg yet. What right do you have to speak?"

"I'm allowed an opinion without laying an egg," said the duckling. The goat stamped its feet and the cat hissed.

"You are only here to be useful. If you can't be useful, at least be quiet," said the goat.

"And while you're at it," said the cat, "you must learn to purr like a cat and produce milk like a goat."

"Why must I?" said the duckling.

"Because we were here first, and this is what we do," said the cat and goat together, in a way that told you they had been saying these words a very long time, so long they no longer really knew what they meant or if they were even true.

"But I can do new things," said the duckling. "I can swim on the surface of the river, and I can dive down into its depths. I can fly. I can—"

"I . . . I . . . I!" said the cat. "You conceited creature. If flying or swimming or diving were useful don't you think one of us would have learned to do it by now?"

The duckling didn't answer because she was filled with such a longing to be in the river and to feel the cool water close over her as she dived down, shutting out the cruel world.

"I think I should go away from here," said the duckling, when she was finally able to speak again. And the goat and cat said, "Yes! Go! You aren't like us, you wrong wrong bill-faced raincloud-feathered flying diving swimming creature."

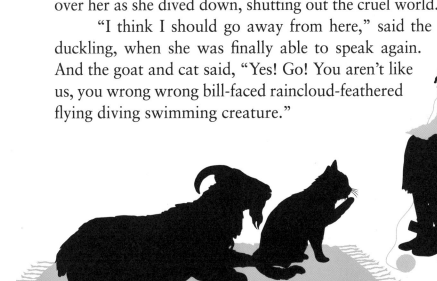

So the duckling left the house and walked toward the direction of the river (somehow she knew where the river was, although she couldn't see it). The ground crunched with fallen leaves, and the air bit at her. It was the end of autumn, and the cold dark days were approaching. As she neared the river, she saw a flock of the most beautiful white birds. Oh, she had never seen anything so lovely as

those long, curved necks and those white white feathers and the grace with which they moved through the water. As she came to the riverbank and was about to call out to them, the swans beat their strong white wings and rose up in the sky, all together, and flew away. She didn't know that swans migrate to warmer climates in the winter and thought it was the sight of the wrong wrong duckling that made them want to flee. She opened her mouth and out came a sound she didn't know she could make, a sound of loneliness and longing. She dived down into the river, and though it was very cold and she was very alone, it brought her some peace to be back in a place that reminded her of her happiest moments, when she swam through a river with her mother, looking for plump eels, and listening to all her mother had to tell her about the world.

As the winter went on, the days turned colder and colder, and soon ice began to form on the river. At first it was just a thin layer on the surface of the water in the early mornings, and it was a game to see how many steps she could take on it before it cracked beneath her weight and she went tumbling in. But the freeze deepened and the ice thickened, closing in over the water from the direction of either bank until there was only a little bit of water uncovered by ice, and the duckling had to swim very rapidly round and round to keep that water from freezing over. Finally, exhausted, she was unable to continue. The ice crept up to her feathers, encircled her feet—and she was stuck fast, unable to move, unable to do anything but shiver with cold and misery.

A farmer walking by saw the stuck duckling and walked carefully onto the iced-over river and used her shoe to break the ice around the duck's feet. She placed the duckling into the inside pocket of her warm jacket and carried her home. But the duckling knew none of this. She had fainted from cold and was unaware of the farmer's act of kindness toward her.

When she woke up, she was in a strange room next to a fire, with pots and pans hanging from the ceiling and the sharp blade of a kitchen knife gleaming in the firelight from its position on a chopping board. The duckling knew there were people who ate any kind of bird they could get their hands on, particularly in the winter when food shortages increased. So when the hands of the farmer reached out for her, she didn't know the woman only wanted to stroke the duckling's feathers and tell her she was safe.

Terrified, the duckling flew up and knocked over a pail of milk, sending its contents spilling onto the floor. The farmer's little son shrieked, which scared the duckling even more, so she started to

fly around blindly just to get away from the hands of the farmer and her son.

CRASH! The plates tumbled out of the drying rack and broke into little pieces.

WHUMP! The side of meat hanging from a hook dislodged and fell to the floor.

THUDDITY-THUDDITY-WAH-WAH-THUDDITY-WAH-THUD-WAAAAAAHHHHH! The basket of garlic and onions rolled over and spilled all its contents onto the child's head.

The front door flung open and the farmer's partner rushed in to see what all the commotion was about. The duckling saw a pathway to the door and, dodging the reaching arms and wooden beams and potted plants, flew out, out and away, far away.

I won't tell you the many sad tales of how the duckling survived the next few months, avoiding all contact with humans and animals and birds. She learned how to keep warm enough and how to eat enough to stay alive, and that was as much as she was capable of doing that long, cold winter.

Eventually spring came around again, and, on a day when it was finally warm enough to bask in the sun and consider the beauty of the light reflecting off water, the duckling saw a large white cloud moving toward her. It came closer and she saw it was the swans returning from their winter migration. Graceful as she remembered, they swooped down to the river and glided along the water as if it was their birthright to be perfectly at home wherever they landed.

The duckling had drawn back into the shadows of a burdock plant when she saw them. But after a short while, she began to ask herself what kind of life she wanted to live. "Must I always hide from the company of others, believing everyone will treat me unkindly? If I do that, I may be safe but I'll be always lonely. Is it better, perhaps, to risk cruelty if it also means taking a chance on kindness?"

The longer she watched the swans, the more she felt the urge for companionship. "Very well," she said to herself, and stepped forward. One step, two steps, three steps, four steps. The swans had noticed her now. They turned their long necks toward her. Her heart beating fast, she stepped into the river, and looking down into the water she saw the most beautiful swan looking back up at her from the river's depths. Oh! Her heart cried out. Who is this under-water swan, and how is it that she's looking at me with the same sense of wonder that I'm showing her?

The other swans on the river glided closer. "Welcome, cousin," one of them said. And "Why haven't we seen you before?" said another. Our duckling looked at the underwater swan again and saw, though she did not yet understand it, that when she moved her wings the swan raised the glory of its own wings; when she bent closer to the surface, the astonishingly elegant creature did the same. It was her reflection. The wrong wrong duckling had grown into a right right swan! She must have changed sometime over the cold, lonely winter, when the frozen river didn't tell her what she looked like.

How can I tell you about her happiness that day? She was welcomed, she was admired, the beauty of her snow-white feathers and her long, curved neck much commented upon. When the swans moved along the river, they took for granted that she would come with them and were astonished that she thought they might leave her behind. When they drifted aimlessly, chewing on the long grass they'd pulled up from the riverbed, she drifted with them, with no need for words.

Days went by in this state of bliss.

Then, one day, a stork hopped along the riverbed toward the swans and said, "Excuse me, could you help me with a search?"

"We are swans," said one of the elder swans. "Why should we help a stork?"

"And one that speaks in such a strange accent, too," giggled a younger swan.

"Look at its spindly legs—how does it even keep upright?" said a third swan, loud enough for the stork to hear.

The raincloud-snow-white-duckling-swan felt a feeling she had never felt in all the months of pain and terror and loneliness and despair. She felt shame. How proud she had been to be admired and accepted by the swans. But creatures who admire you for being just like them are no different from the creatures who mock you for being different. These swans—at least the ones who had spoken— were treating the stork the way the Grand Old Duck and Chablis

Furball and Lofty Cudchew had treated the wrong wrong duckling that she once was.

"I'll help you," she said to the stork. The elder swan who had spoken turned to glare at her, but behind her she heard another elder swan say, "Well done."

"I'm looking for a duck," said the stork. "A duck unlike other ducks. A raincloud-duck, with the heart of a lion, who struck out into the world on her own when other ducklings her age were afraid to go down to the nearest riverbank without their mother."

"What do you want with this duck?" said the duck unlike other ducks.

"Her mother has been searching for her," said the stork. "She asked me to help."

"Why did a duck ask a stork for help?" said the giggling young swan, no longer giggling.

"Because I, too, have been separated from my family," said the stork. "I know the pain of it. And this is more important than my storkness and her duckness."

Our raincloud-snow-white bird felt the words pierce deep into her heart. What did the swans mean by thinking she was just like them? Just like them how? Only in her snow-white feathers and the length of her neck and the size of her webbed feet. But what about her heart, and what about her mind, and what about her spirit?

Later, the mother duck was waiting at the meeting point where she said she'd meet the stork and her two other helpmates at the end of the day when she saw a most unusual sight. The stork was coming toward her down the river, but rather than soaring through the air she was crouched on the head of a swan, her long legs folded up under her, her bill next to the swan's ear.

The stork was telling the swan all that the mother duck had gone through since that awful night when—afraid that the Grand Old Duck would send her and all her ducklings away from the farm just as the first chill of autumn was coming on—she allowed her youngest duckling to be mistreated and joined in the unkindness. "It was only when she saw the duckling fly over the fence into the unknown darkness that she learned what courage looked like," the stork was saying just at the moment the mother duck's heart recognized what her eyes still did not—this swan was her own, her darling, her longed-for and searched-for child.

She cried out with the gladdest cry a duck has ever uttered. The swan cried out in response. They met under a weeping willow, and the duck's wings wrapped fast around the swan's neck.

"My raincloud-duckling," the mother duck said through her tears.

"That is not and never was a duckling," said a stern voice. The other swans had followed the newest of their tribe and the stork to see what was going on, and now the elder swan spoke to the mother duck. "She is a swan. She has always been a swan."

"Perhaps she is both swan and duck," said the stork.

"Neither swan nor duck," said one of the swans.

"Half swan, half duck," said another.

The raincloud-snow-white-duckling-swan swung her neck this way and that, looking at everyone who spoke, trying to know whose words sounded most true.

Then she heard a honking sound. "Hallooo!"

The mother duck's two other helpmates, the brother and sister goslings, now fully grown geese, came sauntering down the riverbed. One had a scar on her cheek that gave her an interesting air, the other had a slight limp that he had transformed into a jaunty hop.

"Don't listen to any of them," said the geese. "You know who you are."

"Yes," said our heroine. "Yes, I do."

"Who are you?" said the mother duck, the stork, and all the swans.

She lifted her wings and beat the air with them. The sky was blue, the water was clear, the world was beautiful and large. She

had survived all the terrible things that had come her way, and she still had a heart to forgive and to love and to want to know who and what lay around the next bend of the river. She raised her neck to the sky and made a sound of power and joy that brought tears to everyone's eyes, even the elder swan.

"I am an adventurer."

Then she turned and looked at the geese, at the duck, at the stork, at the swans, and at you who are reading this story.

"Who's coming with me?" she asked.

AFTERWORD

I can't remember the first time I read or heard "The Ugly Duckling," but I'm fairly sure it was well before I ever saw a picture of a baby swan. I was entirely prepared to believe that cygnets really were ugly until they grew into beautiful swans. But once you've seen a picture of an adorably fluffy cygnet, your way of understanding the story changes. The duckling was never ugly—she (or "he" in the original) was just different. And in the end, when the swans accept and admire her, it is because she has the kind of beauty that is familiar to swans—because it is their kind of beauty. So, settling down to reread Hans Christian Andersen's version of the story before writing my own, I already knew that this was a story about what happens when an outsider enters a homogenous world that is hostile to difference—and then what happens when that same outsider finds "her own tribe" again.

Writers are always on the lookout for magic. Magic can take many forms, but when it comes to an adaptation, it is most commonly found in the shape of something you'd forgotten in the original story that seems to exist in order to tell you that, yes, your new ideas can be grafted onto the old story in a way that makes sense. In my case, this magic appears in the second sentence of Hans Christian Andersen's *The Ugly Duckling*: "The stork walking about on his long red legs chattered in the Egyptian language, which he had learnt from his mother."

This stork never appears in the story again. It's unclear why he's there to begin with. That is to say, it's unclear unless you're about to write a version of "The Ugly Duckling" that is about outsiders—and then it's perfectly clear that the stork of Egyptian heritage, that child of migrants with its foreign language, is there to wave at you across the years and say, yes, go ahead, do it the way you want.

Before I reread "The Ugly Duckling," I remembered it as the story of a creature that met only cruelty until it came upon its fellow swans. Such a story tells you that an outsider will always be mistreated, so you'd better stick with your own kind. But, in fact, the duckling encounters kindness all along the way—most importantly from the mother duck, but also from the goslings and the farmer. I wanted to tell a story in which these acts of love and friendship and kindness helped to form the duckling's character—which is, by the way, a very spirited character. When the cat and hen (which I turned into a goat) tell the duckling to become like them—that is, to assimilate—the duckling stands up for the right to be different and refuses to conform.

All stories, even the ones with timeless qualities, reflect the world we're living in. In our world of hardening borders and increasing suspicion of outsiders, the duckling doesn't offer a different story from the ones around us—rather, she reminds us that in any dark times there are always happier, more generous subplots. We just need to know how to look out for them and how to join in—which is to say, we have to find our inner goslings—so that the subplots become larger and larger and turn into the main story itself.

Copyright © Kamila Shamsie 2020
Illustrations copyright © Laura Barrett 2020

Kamila Shamsie has asserted her right to be identified as the author of this
Work in accordance with the Copyright, Designs and Patents Act 1988

First published by Vintage Classics in 2020
This edition published by Haymarket Books in Chicago in 2021.
Haymarket Books
P.O. Box 180165
Chicago, IL 60618
773-583-7884
www.haymarketbooks.org
info@haymarketbooks.org

A CIP catalogue record for this book is available

ISBN: 978-1-64259-575-8

Distributed to the trade in the US through Consortium Book Sales
and Distribution (www.cbsd.com) and internationally through Ingram
Publisher Services International (www.ingramcontent.com).

This book was published with the generous support of Lannan
Foundation and the Wallace Action Fund.

Special discounts are available for bulk purchases by organizations and
institutions. Please email info@haymarketbooks.org for more information.

Typeset and design by Friederike Huber

Printed in Canada.

2 4 6 8 10 9 7 5 3 1